你要慢慢来，
这本书很危险！

图书在版编目（CIP）数据

穿袜子的狐狸/（美）苏斯著;孙若颖译–北京:中国对外翻译出版公司,2007.1
（苏斯博士双语经典）书名原文:Fox in Fox
ISBN 978-7-5001-1712-4
I.穿… II.①苏…②孙… III.①英语–汉语–对照读物②童话–美国–现代 IV.H319.4:I
中国版本图书馆 CIP 数据核字(2006)第 142733 号

出版发行/中国对外翻译出版公司
地　　址/北京市西城区车公庄大街甲 4 号物华大厦六层
电　　话/(010)68359376 68359303　68359101　68357937
邮　　编/100044
传　　真/(010)68357870
电子邮箱/ctpc@public.bta.net.cn
网　　址/http://www.ctpc.com.cn

策划编辑/李育超 薛振冰 王晓颖
责任编辑/薛振冰 李育超
特约编辑/王甘
责任校对/韩建荣 卓玛
英文朗读/Rayna Martinez Aaron Wickberg & Camila Tamayo
封面设计/大象设计

排　　版/翰文阳光
印　　刷/北京威灵彩色印刷有限公司
经　　销/新华书店

规　　格/787×1092 毫米　1/16
印　　张/4.5
字　　数/15 千字
版　　次/2007 年 4 月第一版
印　　次/2009 年 4 月第四次
印　　数/20 001–23 000

ISBN 978-7-5001-1712-4　定价:19.80 元

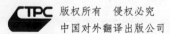

音频下载:登录 http://www.ctpc.com.cn 点击"苏斯博士双语经典"。

　　本书采用了隐形码点读技术,页码所在的椭圆部分置入了隐形码,可配合爱国者点读笔产品点读发音。

Fox in Socks

穿袜子的狐狸

〔美〕Dr. Seuss　图文

孙若颖　译

中国出版集团

中国对外翻译出版公司

★二十世纪最卓越的儿童文学作家之一
★一生创作48种精彩绘本
★作品被翻译成20多种文字和盲文
★全球销量逾2.5亿册
★曾获得美国图画书最高荣誉凯迪克
　大奖和普利策特殊贡献奖
★两次获奥斯卡金像奖和艾美奖
★美国教育部指定的重要阅读辅导读物

I have heard there are troubles of more than one kind. Some come from ahead and some come from behind. But I've bought a big bat. I'm all ready you see. Now my troubles are going to have troubles with me!

我听说人们会有各种各样的麻烦，有的来自前面，有的来自后面。但是我买了一根大球棒。你看，我已经做好准备了，现在我的麻烦要有麻烦了。

——苏斯博士

苏斯是谁?

对于许多美国人而言，他们所能记起的自己所读过的第一本书都出自苏斯博士之手。可以说，在全世界的儿童文学经典作品中，苏斯博士是一座不朽的丰碑。他那绕口令似的韵文、明亮的色彩和充满奇情异想的故事成为一代代孩子的启蒙读物。

苏斯的书有自己显著的标志。只要一看到那些活泼的线条、明朗的画面、幽默的表情，我们马上就知道这些都是苏斯博士的大作。快乐是这些作品最突出的共同特点，苏斯博士没有孩子，他开玩笑说："你拥有他们，而我使他们快乐！"

苏斯博士的书不仅对孩子，而且对大人都有着无穷的魅力，因为它们能带给你最纯粹的快乐。好的图画书不但适合孩子一遍一遍地看，而且适合所有年龄的人看，苏斯博士的书就是这样，直到我们长大甚至老去了，拿起他的书，脸上总会情不自禁地绽出笑容。

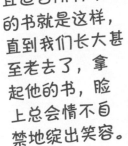

For
Mitzi Long and Audrey Dimond
of the
Mt. Soledad Lingual Laboratories

谨以此书献给
索莱达山语言研究所的米兹·朗和奥德丽·戴蒙德。

Fox

狐狸

Socks

袜子

Box

盒子

Knox

诺克斯

Knox in box.
Fox in socks.

诺克斯在盒子里，
狐狸在袜子里。

Knox on fox
in socks in box.

诺克斯在穿袜子的狐狸上面，
穿袜子的狐狸在盒子里面。

Socks on Knox
and Knox in box.

Fox in socks
on box on Knox.

袜子穿在诺克斯脚上,诺克斯在盒子里面。
穿袜子的狐狸在诺克斯头上的盒子里。

Chicks with bricks come.
Chicks with blocks come.
Chicks with bricks and
blocks and clocks come.

小鸡们带着砖头来了。小鸡们带着积木来了。
小鸡们带着砖头、积木和闹钟来了。

Look, sir. Look, sir.
Mr. Knox, sir.
Let's do tricks with
bricks and blocks, sir.
Let's do tricks with
chicks and clocks, sir.

看啊,先生,看啊。
诺克斯先生,
我们用砖头和积木玩个游戏吧,先生。
我们用小鸡和闹钟玩个游戏吧,先生。

First, I'll make a
quick trick brick stack.
Then I'll make a
quick trick block stack.

首先，我要飞快地把砖头堆起来，
然后再飞快地把积木堆起来。

You can make a
quick trick chick stack.
You can make a
quick trick clock stack.

你可以把小鸡迅速堆起来，
还可以把闹钟迅速堆起来。

And here's a
new trick, Mr. Knox. . . .
Socks on chicks
and chicks on fox.
Fox on clocks
on bricks and blocks.
Bricks and blocks
on Knox on box.

这儿有个新玩法,诺克斯先生……
袜子穿在小鸡脚上,
小鸡站在狐狸身上。
狐狸踩在闹钟上,
闹钟放在砖头和积木上。
砖头和积木架在诺克斯身上,
诺克斯躺在盒子上。

Now we come to
ticks and tocks, sir.
Try to say this
Mr. Knox, sir. . . .

现在我们来玩个嘀嘀和嗒嗒的游戏吧，先生。
试着说说，先生，诺克斯先生……

Clocks on fox tick.
Clocks on Knox tock.
Six sick bricks tick.
Six sick chicks tock.

闹钟在狐狸身上嘀嘀，
闹钟在诺克斯身上嗒嗒。
六块病砖头嘀嘀，
六只病小鸡嗒嗒。

Please, sir. I don't
like this trick, sir.
My tongue isn't
quick or slick, sir.
I get all those
ticks and clocks, sir,
mixed up with the
chicks and tocks, sir.
I can't do it, Mr. Fox, sir.

求你了,先生,
我不喜欢这个游戏,先生。
我口齿不伶俐,先生。
我把嘀嘀嗒嗒,
闹钟和小鸡都弄混了,先生。
我玩不了,狐狸先生。

I'm so sorry,
Mr. Knox, sir.

我很遗憾，诺克斯先生。

Here's an easy
game to play.
Here's an easy
thing to say. . . .

这儿有个容易点儿的游戏可以玩，
这儿有个容易点儿的东西可以说。

New socks.
Two socks.
Whose socks?
Sue's socks.

新袜子，
两只新袜子，
谁的袜子？
苏的袜子。

Who sews whose socks?
Sue sews Sue's socks.

谁缝谁的袜子?
苏缝苏的袜子。

Who sees who sew
whose new socks, sir?
You see Sue sew
Sue's new socks, sir.

谁看见谁缝谁的新袜子,先生?
你看见苏缝苏的新袜子,先生。

That's not easy,
Mr. Fox, sir.

这个不容易呀,狐狸先生。

Who comes? . . .
Crow comes.
Slow Joe Crow comes.

谁来了?⋯⋯
乌鸦来了。
慢性子乌鸦乔来了。

Who sews crow's clothes?
Sue sews crow's clothes.
Slow Joe Crow
sews whose clothes?
Sue's clothes.

谁在缝乌鸦的衣裳？
苏在缝乌鸦的衣裳。
慢性子乌鸦乔在缝谁的衣裳？
在缝苏的衣裳。

Sue sews socks of
fox in socks now.

苏在缝穿袜子的狐狸的袜子。

Slow Joe Crow sews
Knox in box now.

慢性子乌鸦乔把诺克斯缝进了盒子里。

Sue sews rose
on Slow Joe Crow's clothes.
Fox sews hose
on Slow Joe Crow's nose.

苏把玫瑰
缝在慢性子乌鸦乔的衣服上，
狐狸把水管
缝在慢性子乌鸦乔的鼻子上。

Hose goes.
Rose grows.
Nose hose goes some.
Crow's rose grows some.

水管喷呀喷，
玫瑰长呀长。
鼻子上的水管喷一喷，
乌鸦的玫瑰就长一长。

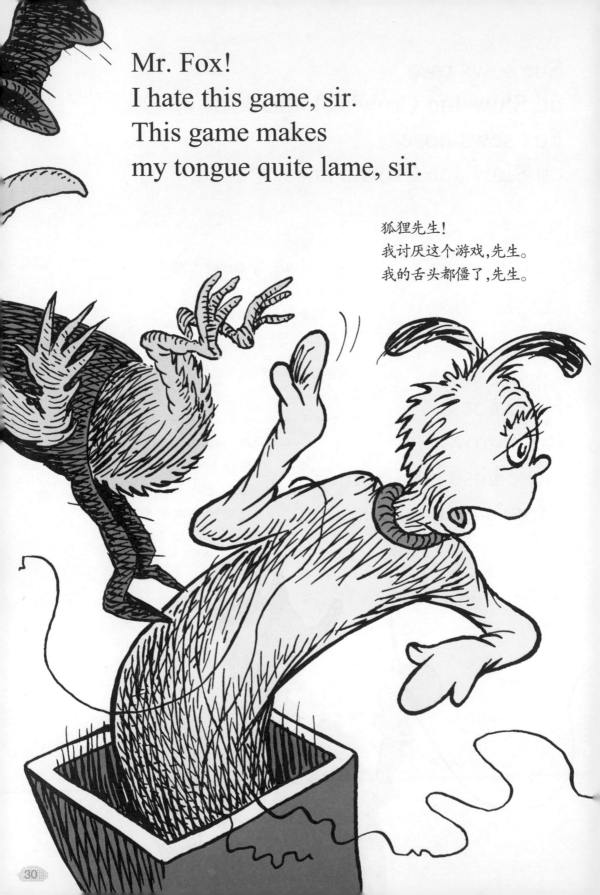

Mr. Fox!
I hate this game, sir.
This game makes
my tongue quite lame, sir.

狐狸先生!
我讨厌这个游戏,先生。
我的舌头都僵了,先生。

Mr. Knox, sir,
what a shame, sir.

诺克斯先生,真遗憾,先生。

We'll find something
new to do now.
Here is lots of
new blue goo now.
New goo. Blue goo.
Gooey. Gooey.
Blue goo. New goo.
Gluey. Gluey.

我们找点新花样儿。
这儿有很多新鲜的蓝胶,
新鲜的胶,蓝色的胶。
粘粘的,稠稠的,
蓝色的胶,新鲜的胶,
稠稠的,粘粘的。

Gooey goo
for chewy chewing!
That's what that
Goo-Goose is doing.
Do you choose to
chew goo, too, sir?
If, sir, you, sir,
choose to chew, sir,
with the Goo-Goose,
chew, sir. Do, sir.

稠稠的胶,
真好咬!
有只鹅
在大嚼。
先生,您也想嚼么?
先生,如果您也想,先生,
就和鹅一起嚼吧,先生。
去嚼吧,先生。

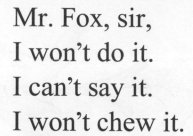

Mr. Fox, sir,
I won't do it.
I can't say it.
I won't chew it.

狐狸先生，
我不想去，
我不会说，
我不想嚼。

Very well, sir.
Step this way.
We'll find another
game to play.

那好吧,先生,
到这边来吧,
我们来玩儿个别的游戏。

Bim comes.
Ben comes.
Bim brings Ben broom.
Ben brings Bim broom.

宾来了，
本来了。
宾给本拿来了扫帚，
本给宾拿来了扫帚。

Ben bends Bim's broom.
Bim bends Ben's broom.
Bim's bends.
Ben's bends.
Ben's bent broom breaks.
Bim's bent broom breaks.

本弄弯了宾的扫帚，
宾弄弯了本的扫帚。
宾的扫帚曲了，
本的扫帚弯了。
本的弯扫帚折了，
宾的弯扫帚断了。

Ben's band. Bim's band.
Big bands. Pig bands.

本的乐队。宾的乐队。
大大乐队。猪猪乐队。

Bim and Ben lead
bands with brooms.
Ben's band bangs
and Bim's band booms.

宾和本
都用扫帚指挥。
本的乐队乒乒，
宾的乐队乒乒。

Pig band! Boom band!
Big band! Broom band!
My poor mouth can't
say that. No, sir.
My poor mouth is
much too slow, sir.

猪猪乐队!热闹的乐队!
大大乐队!扫帚的乐队!
我可怜的嘴巴
说不了那些,不行的,先生。
我可怜的嘴巴
根本跟不上,先生。

Well then. . .
bring your mouth this way.
I'll find it something
it can say.

那好吧……
带上你的嘴巴往这边走。
我来找点儿它能说的东西。

Luke Luck likes lakes.
Luke's duck likes lakes.
Luke Luck licks lakes.
Luke's duck licks lakes.

幸运的勒克喜欢湖，
勒克的鸭子喜欢湖，
幸运的勒克喝湖水，
勒克的鸭子喝湖水。

Duck takes licks
in lakes Luke Luck likes.
Luke Luck takes licks
in lakes duck likes.

鸭子在幸运的勒克喜欢的湖里喝水。
幸运的勒克在鸭子喜欢的湖里喝水。

I can't blab
such blibber blubber!
My tongue isn't
made of rubber.

我说不了这么拗口的句子，
我的舌头不是橡皮做的。

Mr. Knox. Now
come now. Come now.
You don't have to
be so dumb now...

诺克斯先生,
过来,过来。
你现在不必默不作声了……

Try to say this,
Mr. Knox, please. . . .

試着说说这个，
诺克斯先生，求你了……

Through three cheese trees
three free fleas flew.
While these fleas flew,
freezy breeze blew.
Freezy breeze made
these three trees freeze.
Freezy trees made
these trees' cheese freeze.
That's what made these
three free fleas sneeze.

三只跳蚤自由地飞，
飞过三棵奶酪树。
跳蚤飞，
凉风吹。
刺骨的风儿吹呀吹，
树儿冻得颤巍巍。
树上的奶酪结冰啦。
以至于，
三只自由的跳蚤打喷嚏。

Stop it! Stop it!
That's enough, sir.
I can't say
such silly stuff, sir.

别说了！别说了！
够了，先生。
我说不了这些蠢话。

Very well, then,
Mr. Knox, sir.
Let's have a little talk
about tweetle beetles. . . .

那么好吧, 诺克斯先生。
让我们来聊一聊
啾啾叫的甲虫吧……

What do you know
about tweetle beetles?
Well. . .

关于啾啾叫的甲虫
你了解多少？
嗯……

When tweetle beetles fight,
it's called
a tweetle beetle battle.

当啾啾叫的甲虫们打架的时候，
这叫做啾啾甲虫之战。

And when they
battle in a puddle,
it's a tweetle
beetle puddle battle.

而当它们
在水洼里大战的时候，
这叫做啾啾甲虫水洼之战。

AND when tweetle beetles
battle with paddles in a puddle,
they call it a tweetle
beetle puddle paddle battle
                    AND...

而当啾啾叫的甲虫
用木桨在水洼里大战的时候，
他们管这叫啾啾甲虫
水洼木桨之战。
而……

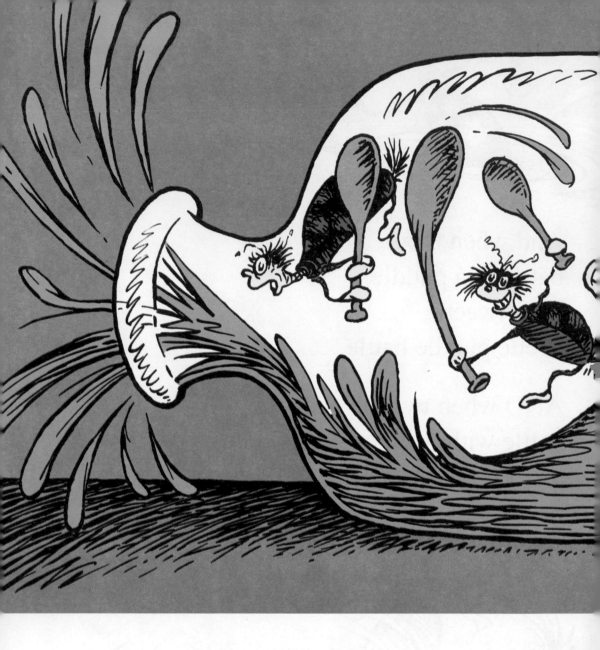

When beetles battle beetles
in a puddle paddle battle
and the beetle battle puddle
is a puddle in a bottle...

当甲虫和甲虫在水洼木桨大战中打仗，
而甲虫大战的水洼是在一个瓶子里的时候……

...they call this
a tweetle beetle
bottle puddle
paddle battle muddle.
                    AND...

……他们管这叫
啾啾甲虫
瓶子水洼
木桨大战泥潭。
而……

When beetles
fight these battles
in a bottle
with their paddles
and the bottle's
on a poodle
and the poodle's
eating noodles...

当甲虫们
在瓶子里
用木桨大战，
而瓶子
落在一只正在吃面条的
卷毛狗背上的时候……

...they call this
a muddle puddle
tweetle poodle
beetle noodle
bottle paddle battle.

                    AND...

……他们管这个叫
泥潭水洼
啾啾卷毛狗
甲虫面条
瓶子木桨之战。
还有……

Now wait
a minute,
Mr. Socks Fox!

等等，穿袜子的狐狸先生！

When a fox is
in the bottle where
the tweetle beetles battle
with their paddles
in a puddle on a
noodle-eating poodle,
THIS is what they call. . .

当狐狸来到瓶子里的时候，
啾啾叫的甲虫们正用木桨
在水洼里大战，
瓶子落在
一只正在吃面条的卷毛狗身上，
这就是他们所说的……

. . .a tweetle beetle
noodle poodle bottled
paddled muddled duddled
fuddled wuddled
fox in socks, sir!

……啾啾甲虫
面条、卷毛狗,装在瓶子里、
被木桨打、
脏兮兮、破烂烂、
糊里糊涂、疯疯癫癫的
穿袜子的狐狸,先生!

Fox in socks,
our game is done, sir.
Thank you for
a lot of fun, sir.

穿袜子的狐狸，
我们的游戏结束了，先生。
谢谢你带给我这么多的欢乐，先生。

阅读提示

苏斯博士,可以说是二十世纪最受欢迎的儿童图画书作家,在英语世界里,是家喻户晓的人物。他创作的图画书,人物形象鲜明,个性突出,情节夸张荒诞,语言妙趣横生,是半个多世纪以来孩子们的至爱,同时他的书也被教育工作者推荐给家长,作为提高阅读能力的重要读物。

孩子喜欢的古怪精灵的读物,为什么也会受到教师的青睐,被列为学生提高阅读能力的重要读物呢?这与苏斯博士开始创作儿童图画书的背景有关。

二十世纪五十年代,美国教育界反思儿童阅读能力低下的状况,认为一个重要原因就是当时广泛使用的进阶型读物枯燥无味,引不起孩子的兴趣。苏斯博士的Beginner Books便应运而生。作为初级阅读资料,这些书力求使用尽可能少的简单词汇,讲述完整的故事。但远远高于过去进阶型读物的,是苏斯博士丰富的想象力、引人入胜的情节和风趣幽默、充满创造力的绘画和语言。

苏斯博士的图画书在讲述有趣故事的同时,更有一个特别的功能,即通过这些故事来使孩子们从兴趣出发轻松地学习英语。从简单的字母,到短语、句子,再到一个个故事,苏斯博士的图画书,亦是一套让孩子们循序渐进掌握英语的优秀读物。例如其中《苏斯博士的ABC》一书,就从英文的二十六个字母入手,将字母和单词配合起来讲解,同时,这些单词又组成了一个个韵味十足的句子,不断重复加深读者对字母的记忆和理解。《一条鱼 两条鱼 红色的鱼 蓝色的鱼》和《在爸爸身上蹦来跳去》也是采取类似的方式进行单词和句子的讲解。《穿袜子的狐狸》则是充满了饶有风趣的绕口令,对诵读者来说是一个充满快乐的挑战。

《绿鸡蛋和火腿》的创作源于苏斯博士和一位朋友打赌，能否用五十个单词写成一个故事。苏斯赢了，于是便有了这本脍炙人口的书。故事是容易引起孩子共鸣的熟悉话题——要不要尝试新食物。故事情节发展激烈，一个拼命劝，一个玩命躲，最后的结局出人意料。苏斯博士的语言是节奏感很强的韵文，朗朗上口，书中所用词汇很少，而且句子结构大量重复，只置换少量单词，孩子一旦记住了第一句，后边的句子很容易读出来，让孩子颇有成就感。

苏斯博士的几本书在几年前曾翻译引入我国，固然读者可以有机会一睹这上世纪儿童文学精品的风采，但语言上的特色在翻译过程中难免有所损失。此次中国对外翻译出版公司采取中英文对照的形式出版苏斯博士的十本书，不仅能让我们能够原汁原味地领略苏斯博士的故事，也是众多小英语学习爱好者的福音。通过韵文学习语言，能增强对语音的辨析能力。更重要的是，苏斯博士令人耳目一新的图画书，能大大增加孩子们学习英语的兴趣，而兴趣是孩子学习的最重要基础。

苏斯博士的书，非常适合大人和孩子一起朗读。

小橡树幼教：王甘博士